THE
TAKING
TREE

a selfish parody

Shrill Travesty
Illustrated by Lucy Ruth Cummins

Simon & Schuster Books for Young Readers
New York London Toronto Sydney

SIMON & SCHUSTER BOOKS FOR YOUNG READERS
An imprint of Simon & Schuster Children's Publishing Division
1230 Avenue of the Americas, New York, New York 10020
For information about special discounts for bulk purchases,
please contact Simon & Schuster Special Sales at
1-866-506-1949 or business@simonandschuster.com.
The Simon & Schuster Speakers Bureau can bring authors to your
live event. For more information or to book an event, contact the
Simon & Schuster Speakers Bureau
at 1-866-248-3049 or visit our website at
www.simonspeakers.com.
Book design by Lucy Ruth Cummins
The text for this book is set in Rockwell.
The illustrations for this book are rendered in
charcoal pencil and watercolor.
Manufactured in China
0710 SCP
2 4 6 8 10 9 7 5 3 1
Library of Congress Cataloging-in-Publication Data
Travesty, Shrill.
The taking tree / Shrill Travesty ;
illustrated by Lucy Ruth Cummins.
p. cm.
ISBN 978-1-4424-0763-3 (hardcover : alk. paper)
1. Boys—Juvenile poetry.
2. Trees—Juvenile poetry.
3. Children's poetry, American.
I. Cummins, Lucy Ruth ill. II. Title.
PS3620.R375T35 2010
811'.6—dc22
2009043104

To my old gang from BEHS—
Barry, Mike, P. J., Elisa, and Paul
—S. T.
For my army of nieces
—L. R. C.

Once there was a kid who spent every day under a tree.

The tree was his best friend.

Which shows what a
loser the kid was.

The kid used to take twigs from the tree
and poke his sister with them.

And he took acorns from the tree to whip at old people.

And he carved things in the tree . . .

. . . that he almost instantly regretted.

The kid was a real jerk.

The tree just hated the kid.
But she couldn't get away from him.
She was a tree.
This was where her roots were.

One day the kid took leaves from
the tree and started some small fires
with them.

And one not-so-small fire.

And the kid went away for a very long time. . . .

And the tree was very happy.

And so were her friends.
A pine tree told her,
"Girlfriend, that kid is a dog."

There is nothing trees hate more than dogs.

Many years later the kid came back.
But he was not a kid anymore. He was a teenager.
Meaning he was an even bigger jerk.

He told the tree, "I want to go away to college, but I have no money to pay for it. Will you give me your apples?"

The tree said, "I'm an oak tree. I can't grow apples. When have you ever seen me grow apples?"

And the kid whined, "Come on. I thought you were my friend."

"There's an apple tree right over there," said the tree.

"Quit stalling," said the kid.

"Is there even a college that takes apples as tuition?" asked the tree.

"Just do it," said the kid.

And to shut the kid up,
the tree actually managed
to grow apples.

It was not easy.

When she was done, the kid said, "You can keep your apples. I just got a scholarship."

"Oh, man," said the tree.

The boy went away for a very long time.

And the tree was very happy . . .

. . . until he came back.

Now he was no longer a kid.

He was a very successful businessman.

Which often happens when little jerks
grow up.

And the kid said, "I would like to take
your branches and build a beautiful
home right here in the forest."

And the tree said, "Gosh, I really need
my branches . . . and there's a big pile of
bricks over there that you could use. . . ."

The kid didn't even listen. He was
already snapping off her branches.

And he built a little house right next
to her.

"Oh, nuts," said the tree.

The next day the house burned down.

The tree was very happy . . .

. . . until she found out the kid
survived the fire.

In fact, he had insured the
little house for five million
dollars.

For some reason.

And the kid came to the tree with two suitcases bulging
with money.

And he said, "I need to get out of here, and I'm in kind of
a hurry. Can I cut you down and carve your trunk into a
canoe?"

And the tree said
to the kid she had
known for so long . . .

"Are you out of your mind?

"You took my branches, you took my twigs, you took my acorns, you took my leaves, you even took my apples— wherever those came from.

"You took everything you could take. And I can't take it anymore!"

Then the tree took the kid's hat and threw it in the river.

And she took the kid's credit cards and ordered a bunch of DVDs she had no intention of watching.

And she took the kid's cell phone and called the cops.

"How do you like them apples?" said the tree.

And the kid went
away for a very, very,
very long time.

And the tree was really, really happy.

One day the kid came back. But he was not a kid anymore. He was an old man.

And he said, "When I got out of jail, I could not get my old job back."

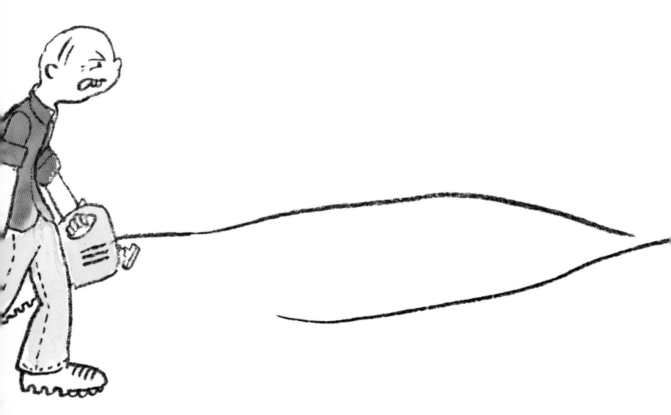

And the tree said,
"Oh, boo-hoo. I'm a
weeping willow."

"I am no longer a businessman. Now I am a lumberman."

And the kid took out a big chain saw.

The tree began to sweat, which no tree has ever done, before or since.

She said, "Hey, remember the fun we used to have, back in—"

The kid could not hear the rest.
The chain saw made too much noise.
And when he cut completely
through her trunk . . .

. . . the tree fell on him.

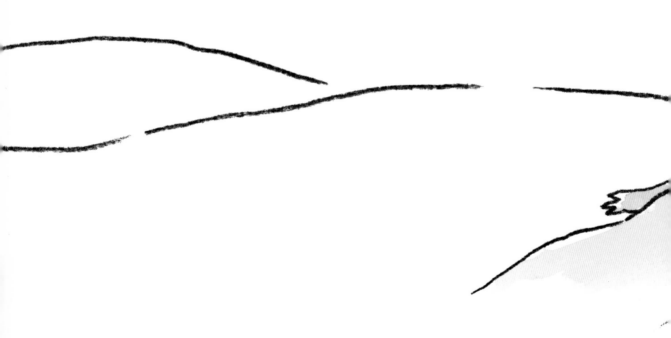

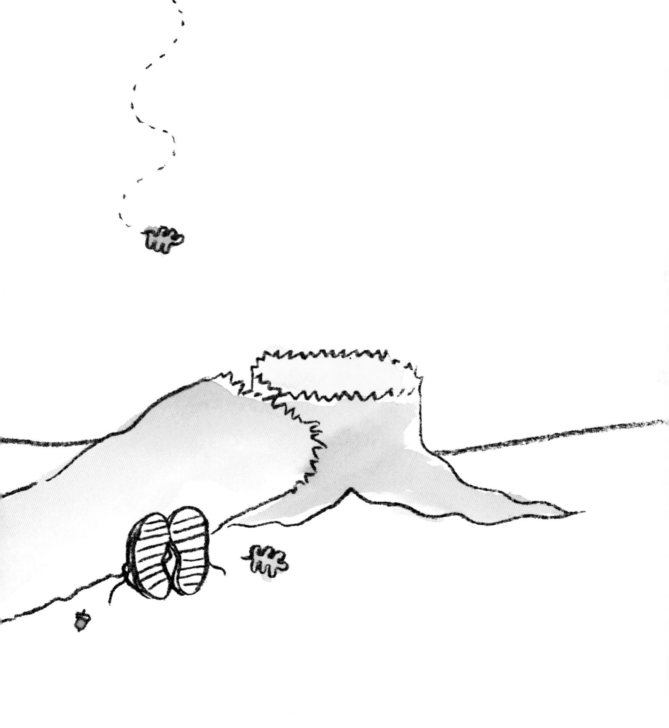

Now the kid spends every day under the tree. . . .

I have no idea if the tree is happy about this or not.

The trunk of the tree was made into paper.
They printed a book on it.
You just read it.